Jeremy Strong once worked in a bakery, putting the jam into three thousand doughnuts every night. Now he puts the jam in stories instead, which he finds much more exciting. At the age of three, he fell out of a first-floor bedroom window and landed on his head. His mother says that this damaged him for the rest of his life and refuses to take any responsibility. He loves writing stories because he says it is 'the only time you alone have complete control and can make anything happen'. His ambition is to make you laugh (or at least snuffle). Jeremy Strong lives near Bath with his wife, Gillie, four cats and a flying cow.

Are you feeling silly enough to read more?

THE BATTLE FOR CHRISTMAS
THE BEAK SPEAKS
BEWARE! KILLER TOMATOES
CHICKEN SCHOOL
DINOSAUR POX
GIANT JIM AND THE HURRICANE
I'M TELLING YOU, THEY'RE ALIENS
THE INDOOR PIRATES
THE INDOOR PIRATES ON TREASURE ISLAND
INVASION OF THE CHRISTMAS PUDDINGS
THE KARATE PRINCESS
THE KARATE PRINCESS TO THE RESCUE
KRAZY COW SAVES THE WORLD – WELL, ALMOST
LET'S DO THE PHARAOH!
PANDEMONIUM AT SCHOOL
PIRATE PANDEMONIUM
THE SHOCKING ADVENTURES OF LIGHTNING LUCY
THERE'S A PHARAOH IN OUR BATH!
THERE'S A VIKING IN MY BED AND OTHER STORIES
TROUBLE WITH ANIMALS

Read about Streaker's adventures:
THE HUNDRED-MILE-AN-HOUR DOG
RETURN OF THE HUNDRED-MILE-AN-HOUR DOG
WANTED! THE HUNDRED-MILE-AN-HOUR DOG
LOST! THE HUNDRED-MILE-AN-HOUR DOG

Read about Nicholas's daft family:
MY DAD'S GOT AN ALLIGATOR!
MY GRANNY'S GREAT ESCAPE
MY MUM'S GOING TO EXPLODE!
MY BROTHER'S FAMOUS BOTTOM
MY BROTHER'S FAMOUS BOTTOM GETS PINCHED
MY BROTHER'S FAMOUS BOTTOM GOES CAMPING
MY BROTHER'S HOT CROSS BOTTOM

JEREMY STRONG'S LAUGH-YOUR-SOCKS-OFF
JOKE BOOK

LAUGH YOUR SOCKS OFF WITH

Jeremy
STRONG

There's a
PHARAOH
in our Bath!

Illustrated by
Nick
Sharratt

PUFFIN

PUFFIN BOOKS

Published by the Penguin Group
Penguin Books Ltd, 80 Strand, London WC2R 0RL, England
Penguin Group (USA) Inc., 375 Hudson Street, New York, New York 10014, USA
Penguin Group (Canada), 90 Eglinton Avenue East, Suite 700, Toronto, Ontario, Canada M4P 2Y3
(a division of Pearson Penguin Canada Inc.)
Penguin Ireland, 25 St Stephen's Green, Dublin 2, Ireland (a division of Penguin Books Ltd)
Penguin Group (Australia), 250 Camberwell Road, Camberwell, Victoria 3124, Australia
(a division of Pearson Australia Group Pty Ltd)
Penguin Books India Pvt Ltd, 11 Community Centre, Panchsheel Park, New Delhi – 110 017, India
Penguin Group (NZ), 67 Apollo Drive, Rosedale, North Shore 0632, New Zealand
(a division of Pearson New Zealand Ltd)
Penguin Books (South Africa) (Pty) Ltd, 24 Sturdee Avenue, Rosebank, Johannesburg 2196, South Africa

Penguin Books Ltd, Registered Offices: 80 Strand, London WC2R 0RL, England

puffinbooks.com

First published by Dutton 1995
Published in Puffin Books 1997
This edition published 2009 for The Book People Ltd,
Hall Wood Avenue, Haydock, St Helens, WA11 9UL
1

Text copyright © Jeremy Strong, 1995
Illustrations copyright © Nick Sharratt, 1995
All rights reserved

The moral right of the author and illustrator has been asserted

Set in Baskerville
Made and printed in England by Clays Ltd, St Ives plc

British Library Cataloguing in Publication Data
A CIP catalogue record for this book is available from the British Library

ISBN: 978-0-141-32789-1

www.greenpenguin.co.uk

Penguin Books is committed to a sustainable future
for our business, our readers and our planet.
The book in your hands is made from paper
certified by the Forest Stewardship Council.

Contents

1 A Surprise from the Past

The lid of the cobwebbed coffin was slowly
pushed back and the two men laid it
carefully on the museum floor. They stared
inside at the beautifully painted Ancient
Egyptian mummy-case, covered with
picture-writing.

Daylight was already beginning to fade from the musty store-room. The other museum staff had long since gone home and the only company left with the two men now were stacks of old mummy-cases, ancient skeletons and a large, stuffed rhinoceros.

Professor Jelly pulled the lamp closer and inspected the hieroglyphs. The light shimmered across his moon-like face, making the pearls of sweat on his brow sparkle like tiny jewels.

'What does it say?' demanded Grimstone. The head of the museum's Ancient Egyptian collection stared over Jelly's shoulder. 'Is it the mummy of the missing Pharaoh?'

Professor Jelly took a sweet from his jacket-pocket, popped it in his mouth and bent over the mummy-case. 'Hmmmm, hazelnut crunch. Now, this squiggly bit here says MAY PERFUMED FLOWERS BE CRUSHED BENEATH HIS

FEET. Very poetic.'

'But who's inside?' Grimstone barked impatiently, and his great winged eyebrows crashed together over his hooded eyes and hawk-nose. He stabbed a thin finger at one side of the coffin. 'What about here? What does this say? It looks important.'

Professor Jelly sucked noisily on his sweet. 'That bit there?'

'Yes!'

'That says PLEASE KEEP THIS WAY UP AT ALL TIMES.'

'What!' yelled Grimstone.

'And that bit,' continued the professor, waving at some faded hieroglyphs with a pudgy hand, 'that bit there says NOT TO BE OPENED BEFORE CHRISTMAS.'

For a few seconds Grimstone was stunned, then his eyes glinted dangerously. 'You're making this up, Jelly, aren't you?'

The professor straightened his tubby frame. 'Of course I'm making it up. Stop pestering me and let me study it properly. This mummy has been stuck here for seventy years already, ever since it was first brought to the museum from Ancient Egypt for the collection. A few more minutes' wait won't hurt.'

Once again, Professor Jelly bent his glistening bald head over the mummy-case, while Grimstone strode angrily around the cramped room, until he came face to face with the stuffed rhino. 'And *you* can stop staring too!' hissed Grimstone. 'This could be the discovery of the century. It could make our fortunes. We *could* be millionaires. The clue to a fabulous treasure is in that coffin.' He turned back to the professor. 'Come on, Jelly, get a move on.'

The professor was still translating the hieroglyphs on the coffin's side. 'HE WHO OPENS THIS COFFIN WILL BE CURSED BY ANUBIS. There now, just our luck. We're going to be cursed by Anubis.'

'Who's Anubis?' demanded Grimstone.

'He was the Ancient Egyptian God of the Dead – had a head like a jackal.'

'And what kind of curses did he make?'

'Oh, usual sort of thing – may your body be devoured by giant ants for a thousand years; may your heart be torn from your rib-cage by crocodiles . . .' Jelly popped another sweet into his mouth.

Grimstone had turned pale. 'Do the curses work?'

'No idea,' replied Jelly. 'Nobody has ever lived to say. Ah, listen to this!' his voice rose with excitement. '**HERE LIES THE MOST SACRED BODY OF THE ROYAL PHARAOH WHOSE NAME SHALL RUMBLE DOWN THE AGES.** It's him! It's Sennapod, the missing Pharaoh from the Four-fifths Dynasty!'

The two men grinned madly, grasped each other by the hands and began to waltz around the room, crashing into old mummy-cases and sending clouds of dust into the eerie gloom. 'We'll be rich!' yelled Grimstone.

'We'll be famous!' cried Jelly.

'Sennapod,' panted Grimstone, coming to a halt. 'Known to the Ancient Egyptians as

He Whose Name Shall Rumble Down The
Ages. We know from Ancient Egyptian
writings that a massive treasure was buried
near his tomb and a map showing its
location was hidden in the coffin. Nobody
has ever found the coffin – until now! Can
you find the map, Jelly?'

'We shall have to open the mummy-case.
What about the curse?'

'Curse the curse! What about the treasure?' snapped Grimstone.

The two men gingerly levered open the lid, sweating with the effort. The cold silence was broken only by their grunts. From every side they were watched by the unblinking painted eyes of dead priests and Ancient Egyptian princes. They lifted the lid from the base and there he was – Sennapod, over four thousand years old and wrapped entirely in rather smelly, yellow bandages.

Grimstone clapped one hand across his face and staggered back. 'Phew – he does pong.'

'So would you if you'd been dead that long,' Professor Jelly pointed out. 'But look, Sennapod is holding some parchment. It must be the map!' The professor gently pulled the ancient paper from between the mummy's stiff, bandaged fingers. It crackled as it was unfolded and little pieces broke from the edge and drifted to the floor. Professor Jelly held it to the light, cleared his throat and began to read. '**FROM THE LAND OF THE WEST, THE GREAT AND SERENE GODS OF ANCIENT EGYPT GREET SENNAPOD, KING OF THE NILE, LORD OF SERPENTS, MASTER OF HIPPOPOTAMUSES** . . .'

'Master of hippopotamuses?' repeated Grimstone. 'Are you making that up?'

Professor Jelly shook his head. 'The Ancient Egyptians always put in things like that. It made them feel important.' The professor scrutinized the centuries-old message. The room suddenly grew darker and much colder. The upright stacks of coffins seemed to close in around the two men. Jelly shuddered and went on. 'Listen: FROM THE LAND OF THE WEST, THE GREAT GODS OF EGYPT SPIT UPON THE WORM WHO IS READING THE SECRET CURSE. THOU HAST BROKEN THE SEAL OF THE PHARAOH SENNAPOD AND LITTERED HIS SLEEPING PLACE WITH THINE WORM-LIKE PRESENCE. EVEN AS THINE WORM-EYES READ THIS CURSE, SENNAPOD WILL ARISE BEFORE YOU AND STRIKE YOU DOWN – THOU WORM –'

'They didn't like worms much, did they?' put in Grimstone, but Professor Jelly carried on reading.

'HE IS THE MIGHTY WARRIOR WHO MUST BE OBEYED. HIS IS THE NAME THAT SHALL RUMBLE DOWN THE AGES. HE IS THE RISEN OSIRIS AND HIS CAT IS THE . . .'

Jelly's voice died in his throat. Something was gripping his arm fiercely. It was Grimstone, clinging to the professor with one hand and pointing, horror-struck, at the coffin with the other. Even as the two men trembled and stared, transfixed with terror, they saw the mummy in the case begin to twitch . . .

The yellow fingers moved.

The bandaged mouth struggled open and fresh air hissed into the ancient lungs as they began to breathe once more.

The head lifted with a jerk and the body sat up. One leg raised itself from the coffin and the mummy slowly rose to its feet, with

bandages falling away and
trailing to the floor.

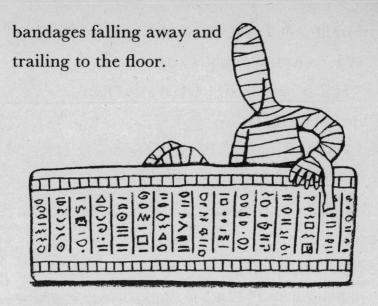

Grimstone and Jelly tried to scream. They
opened their mouths, but their voices had
run so far away, they were impossible to
find. The men tried to escape, but their feet
were rooted to the ground. They stared at
each other, stared back at the advancing
mummy, tried to climb up each other and
fell to the floor in a gibbering heap.

The Pharaoh Sennapod, Lord of Serpents,
Master of Hippos and Crusher of Worms,
stepped over the quaking bodies, crashed

through the door and stumbled out into the dark and rainy night.

It just happened to be his 4,600th birthday.

2 Roast Hippo and Chips

Sennapod fumbled at the rain-soaked
bandages round his face, trying to see where

he was going. He had
already walked into
three lamp-posts and
a litter-bin. At last, a
pair of bottomless
eyes, glistening like
two frozen stones,
stared despairingly
into the gloom.

Sennapod was
lost. This
was hardly

surprising. He had been asleep for the last
four thousand or so years and the world had
changed quite a lot. He seemed to remember
being buried deep inside some pyramid, on

the edge of a great desert, but this didn't
look like a desert at all. There was no sand,
no sun, and it was raining.

A small tabby cat
paused for a moment
and watched the strange,
pale figure stagger
towards it. Instead of
dashing for cover, the
cat trotted over, gave
a tiny mew and leaped

lightly into Sennapod's arms. The Pharaoh's
eyes glinted with pleasure. So, cats still came
to him, even after all these centuries. He
gently put the tabby down and stumbled on.

His head ached furiously, as if several
gigantic pyramid blocks were being dragged
around inside it. He felt weak and his legs
wobbled. He had not eaten for forty
centuries, and now he was starving.

Just then, he saw a white van parked by

 the roadside. There were pictures of food painted on the outside. Above the big side-window was a sign that said MISTER FREEZEE. Next to the window was a poster showing different ice-lollies, hot-dogs, burgers and chips.

Inside the van, Tony Lightspeed was snoring comfortably in the driver's seat, blissfully unaware that a very wet Ancient Egyptian Pharaoh was slowly getting closer and closer. Sennapod stopped and tried to focus his four-thousand-year-old eyes on the poster. The pictures on it swam before him. His legs felt like damp towels and he knew they wouldn't hold him up much longer. He needed food! The Pharaoh banged impatiently on the counter of the van.

Mr Lightspeed stirred in his seat and

pushed back his battered baseball cap. 'Oh, sorry – didn't hear you coming, what with all this rain we're having. Dreadful isn't it?' He struggled through to the back of the van. 'Now then, sir, what can I get you?' Tony Lightspeed glanced at his customer for the first time and his eyes froze. He felt he was gazing at Death himself.

Sennapod struggled to speak the first words he had uttered since 2551 BC. A thin, dry, sand-blasted voice crackled inside his throat and his grey lips parted. 'I want a

roast hippopotamus
stuffed with figs
and dates, three
lots of French
fries, no ketchup –
and a slice of birthday
cake.' He glared back
at Mr Lightspeed's astonished
face. 'You are nothing but a small worm,'
he added for good measure. Then his
eyes rolled slowly upwards and he sank
unconscious into a puddle.

'Well, I never!' exclaimed Mr Lightspeed,
leaning right out of his van and gazing with
concern down at the soggy Pharaoh. He
hurried out and tried to lift Sennapod to his
feet.

'Urgh, you're soaking. We'd better get
you somewhere warm and dry. You'll catch
your death out here in this weather. Come
on, into the van.' Mr Lightspeed opened the

passenger door and, with a good deal of grunting, somehow managed to heave, shove and poke the Pharaoh into the seat. He pulled the seat-belt round his ancient passenger and buckled it. A few moments later the van was on the move and Mr Lightspeed turned his cheerful, wrinkled face towards Sennapod.

'As soon as we get you home, you're going to change out of those wet things. Fancy going about dressed like that! We'll run you a nice hot bath and find some dry clothes. Eve – that's my wife – she'll knock you up some grub. You mustn't mind if the kids are a bit noisy – you know what kids are like. Carrie and Ben, that's my two. Fourteen and nine. You're very quiet, aren't you?'

Sennapod's head lolled forwards. 'Oh, sorry! You're still unconscious. Perhaps we ought to call a doctor? Look, here we are, 27 Templeton Terrace.' As the van came to a

halt, so did Mr Lightspeed's one-way
conversation. He undid the seat-belt, hoisted
the Pharaoh over one broad shoulder in a
fireman's lift and carried him up the path
and into the narrow house.

'Make way, make way,' he cried, barging
into the cramped front room. 'We've got a
visitor, and he's a bit out of sorts.' Mr
Lightspeed tipped Sennapod into an

armchair, where he landed with a large squelch.

Mrs Lightspeed was so surprised she put the banana that she was about to peel straight into her mouth, skin and all. She was built on a big scale, and the banana made her look like a startled toucan. Ben and Carrie looked at each other and shrugged. Dad was always bringing something home. One week it was an injured owl. Another time it was a stray dog; now he'd somehow managed to rescue a whole person.

Eve Lightspeed quickly pulled the banana from her mouth. 'He's soaking, Tony, and why has he got all those bandages on?'

Carrie grunted. 'That's obvious, isn't it? Ben's been practising his First Aid again.'

'Don't be so silly, Carrie,' said Mrs Lightspeed, pulling long strips from Sennapod's head and wringing them out.

'Well, he bandaged up next-door's cat last week, didn't he? And our goldfish.'

'I never!' yelled Ben. 'You're making it up! She's making it up, Mum, honest.'

Carrie, who nearly always looked perfect because of the vast amount of time she spent preening herself, grinned at her mop-haired brother, delighted that she had managed to get him so worked up.

'I bet he saw this poor man asleep,' she went on relentlessly. 'He whipped out his box of bandages – Ben's Big Bumper Box of Bandages – that's what he calls it . . .'

'I don't! I don't!' cried Ben, trying to smother his sister with two large cushions.

'All right, you two,' snapped Mr

Lightspeed, anxiously watching his wife.

Mrs Lightspeed was fussing over the
Pharaoh. She was very worried to see how
grey and wrinkled Sennapod's face was
beneath the wrappings. 'He's got a dreadful
skin complaint, Tony. I think I'll get some
moisturizing cream for him. And his hair
needs a good wash. It's all sticky and
matted. He does look a bit gruesome, don't
you think?'

'Maybe he's from the hospital,' suggested
Mr Lightspeed. 'That would explain all the

bandages. Ben – I think Carrie has stopped breathing. Could you stop sitting on her head?'

But the all-out battle raging between the two children might well have continued for several more minutes, possibly even years, if Sennapod had not chosen that moment to wake.

The Pharaoh sat bolt upright, his

haunting eyes fixing on all four of them at once with a commanding glare. Ben was almost certain he could see little red dots shooting out of Sennapod's eyes which seemed to burn into his body, but it might just have been his imagination. The Pharaoh lifted a bony, half-bandaged arm and pointed at the Lightspeed family.

'Worms!' he roared, by way of saying hello. 'Do you dare raise your voices in front of the Pharaoh! Do you dare wage your puny wars before *me*!' Sennapod struggled to his feet. 'I am He Whose Name Shall Rumble Down The Ages. You are mere maggots and slugs, to be squeezed between my fingers – like so! I have been dead over four thousand years – bring me food at once!' The effort of this speech left Sennapod very weak and he sank back into the armchair with another loud squelch.

Mrs Lightspeed vanished into the little

kitchen and began to make a pile of cheese sandwiches. It was not that she was scared of Sennapod, but she simply could not bear to think of anyone who hadn't eaten for that long. Poor man – didn't he have *anyone* to look after him? Mr Lightspeed looked as if he might ask something, but then he hurried after his wife and nervously began buttering bread for her. That left Ben and Carrie alone with the mummy.

'Are you really a Pharaoh?' asked Ben, much to Sennapod's astonishment.

'Are you speaking to *me*?' he demanded with scandalized disgust. 'Worms must be silent, and only speak when spoken to.'

Ben frowned. 'Could you stop calling me a worm, please? Mum says it's rude to call people names – unless it's your sister, of course. You can call her anything you like.'

Carrie scowled and turned to Sennapod. 'If you've been dead over four thousand years,' she said, 'how come you're alive now?'

'A miserable maggot must have read The Curse of Anubis,' sneered Sennapod.

Carrie was bewildered. 'A nudist?' she asked, wondering what sort of curses nudists might make.

Ben sighed heavily. 'He didn't say a nudist, Carrie. He said Anubis, the Ancient Egyptian God of the Dead. Don't you know *anything*?' He peered at the Pharaoh in the armchair. Something about Sennapod's appearance made Ben wonder. Perhaps he really was an Ancient Egyptian. That would be incredible!

'I hope you like cheese,' said Mr Lightspeed, coming back from the kitchen with a large plate of sandwiches. 'Very good for your energy levels. Now, what's this about a nudist? You're not going to take any more bandages off, surely?'

Ben could see that Sennapod was totally

bewildered by both Carrie and his father. He tried to explain yet again, while the Pharaoh eagerly crammed his grey mouth with the sandwiches. 'Anubis, Dad. He had tall pointy ears and a long pointy nose, very similar to Carrie's.'

'Did he really?' said Carrie icily. 'Ha, ha, ha.'

'No, not really. Actually yours is much longer.'

'Oh – double ha ha,' Carrie growled.

'How do you know all this, Ben?' asked Mrs Lightspeed.

'Well, you only have to look at her,' said Ben.

'No! About Anubis.'

'We're doing the Ancient Egyptians at school,' he answered.

Mr Lightspeed's face puckered into a frown, and he eyed Sennapod warily. 'Are you trying to tell me that this person here is a dead Ancient Egyptian?'

Ben burst out laughing. 'Don't be daft, Dad. He wouldn't be here if he was dead. This person is a *living* Ancient Egyptian!'

For a moment there was a stunned silence, then Mrs Lightspeed took a deep breath. 'I think we had better ask Mister Pharaoh here to explain himself,' she said. But Sennapod had slumped back into a semi-coma, overcome by the effort of being alive once more – not to mention trying to cope with all the Lightspeeds. His grey face had tipped to one side and his eyes were firmly shut. He did not look at all well.

'We'd better take him upstairs and put him in Carrie's bed,' said Mr Lightspeed.

'My bed! Why not Ben's?'

'Have you seen Ben's bed?' asked her

mother. 'It's not a bed at all. It's a pig-bin. You can put the air-bed on our floor tonight, Carrie. There's no room anywhere else.'

They lifted the Pharaoh from the armchair and carefully carried him upstairs and put him in Carrie's bed. Explanations would have to wait until morning.

3 The Chase Begins

Meanwhile, back at the museum, more strange things had been taking place. Lying unnoticed in a corner of Sennapod's old coffin was another mummy. It was small, had four legs and a long tail and two pointed ears, all neatly bandaged. The mini-mummy stretched itself slowly, arching its back. It gave a muffled miaow and jumped lightly out of the coffin.

The two confused and terrified bodies lying on the floor had also come back to life. Grimstone scrambled to his feet and grabbed Professor Jelly. They peered out through the shattered door.

'Sennapod is alive!' muttered Grimstone.

'He's out there, somewhere – a real Four-fifths Dynasty Ancient Egyptian Pharaoh, roaming the streets.'

Professor Jelly buried his bald head in both hands. 'I've got a massive headache,' he mumbled. 'I don't remember anything in The Curse of Anubis about a headache, do you?'

'Who cares about headaches?' cried

Grimstone. 'Don't you understand? We've got a real Pharaoh on our hands and he's wandering about out there with the treasure map – *our* map, Jelly – unless he left it here, of course.' Grimstone scrabbled around inside the mummy-case. 'I can't see anything in here, can you?'

Professor Jelly ran his piggy eyes around the painted interior, slowly translating the hieroglyphs. 'There's nothing about treasure. Ah – that explains it,' he sighed.

'What? Have you found the key to the treasure?'

'No, but you see those signs there? They say HE WHO OPENS THE TOMB OF SENNAPOD SHALL HAVE A HEAD THAT FEELS LIKE A CEMENT MIXER.'

Grimstone wasn't the least bit interested in the professor's headache. He tried to pull his colleague away, but only managed to trip over a completely bandaged cat that seemed to have appeared from nowhere. 'Good heavens! What on earth?' The cat rubbed its head against Grimstone's leg.

Professor Jelly bent down and picked it up. 'Well now, just look at this, Grimstone.' The professor fingered the small, ancient clay tablet hanging round the cat's neck. He read the hieroglyphs. 'This is Sennapod's personal cat, Crusher of Worms. The curse must have woken him too.'

Grimstone snarled, tweaked his beaky nose, and walked quickly to the door. Cats always made him sneeze. 'We've no time for pussy-cats, Jelly. If the map isn't here, then that festering Pharaoh must have it. We must find him, and it shouldn't be too difficult. Put that cat down and hurry up.' He bellowed back to his colleague. 'Can't you walk any faster?'

'I've got short legs. It's not my fault I've

got short legs. *And* I've got a headache.'

'Stop moaning!' cried Grimstone. 'Somewhere out on the streets is a fortune walking around in stinky bandages.'

The two men hurried through the revolving main doors of the empty museum and stood outside on the wet steps, peering into the rain. Professor Jelly hated the rain. With no hair on his head to help soak it up, the drops ran straight off his shiny skull and dribbled down his neck.

'He could still be inside,' the professor pointed out hopefully, as he locked the museum doors. But Grimstone stalked down the steps and plucked a piece of sodden bandage from the pavement. He held it up triumphantly. 'Look, it's Sennapod's. There's no time to lose. You take your bicycle. I'll go on my moped. We'll comb the streets. We're bound to find him.'

Grimstone ran to the car-park, dragging

Jelly behind. A few moments later, a small engine sputtered into life and Grimstone set off, his spidery body dwarfing the rather wobbly moped beneath his bony backside. A bell tinkled in the darkness and Professor Jelly appeared, on an even more wobbly bicycle.

Professor Jelly began to pedal wearily up

and down the silent back streets, squinting into the shadowy corners and calling. 'Mummy? Mummy? Where are you? Come to me – come to daddy. Oh dear, what am I saying?'

The two hunters disappeared into the streets surrounding the museum, four eyes piercing the gloom as they set about tracking down their fortune.

4 Burglars!

Strange noises were coming from downstairs. Ben stirred and woke. It was early morning and the sun filtered lazily through his curtains. Ben glanced at the clock. Five-thirty! What was going on? BANG! CRASH! Something heavy was being dragged about downstairs. Ben's heart began to pound loudly. It must be burglars!

He pushed back the covers, pulled on his dressing-gown and crept to the door. He quietly pulled it open. The thuds and scrapes continued, with a lot of grunting as well. Maybe there were two of them! Ben glanced up the hallway. Carrie's door was still shut. He slipped across to his parents' room and carefully opened their door. They were fast asleep. Dad was still wearing his baseball cap. He must warn them!

Ben took four steps into the dark bedroom, trod on something large and squashy, then fell on top of it. Carrie let out a very crumpled squeak and angrily pushed Ben away. 'What are you . . . ?'

'Ssssh!' hissed Ben. 'Sorry, I forgot you were in here. Listen, there are burglars downstairs.' Carrie was about to say something very sarcastic when a loud crash from below made her sit up at once. She stared at Ben, round-eyed. 'I'm going to tell Dad,' he said, and he hurried to his father and began shaking him.

Carrie woke her mother and all four of them listened to the thuds and grunts. Stealthily, they crept down the stairs, with Dad and Mum at the front. Mr Lightspeed was carrying his old guitar high above his head, ready to batter any burglar they came across.

Just as they reached the door to the front room, the bumps and thumps stopped. An eerie silence followed. 'Now's our chance,' whispered Mr Lightspeed, pulling his baseball cap down firmly. 'When I say "go", we all rush in. OK?'

Mrs Lightspeed clutched her husband's arm. 'When you say "go",' she repeated, and turned to Ben and Carrie. 'When your dad says "go", we all rush in,' she explained nervously, as if they hadn't already heard.

Mr Lightspeed shuffled his feet. 'I'm going to say "go" any second,' he warned. 'Ready?'

'Ready,' said Ben and Carrie.

'Ready,' said Mrs Lightspeed.

Mr Lightspeed gripped his guitar even more tightly. 'Right, then, here we go . . .' He was about to shout 'go', but the other three thought he'd just given the command, and with a blood-curdling yell three Lightspeeds rushed forward.

Mr Lightspeed was knocked flat on his face, while his wife and children trampled

straight over him and burst into the front room. There was a loud TWANG! as Ben put one foot through his father's guitar. It flapped around his foot like a gigantic wooden slipper.

Mr Lightspeed struggled to his feet, to find his wife and Ben and Carrie standing in the front room, goggling thunderstruck.

Right on top of the dining table was an armchair, and sitting majestically in the armchair was He Whose Name Shall Rumble Down The Ages. Sennapod's arms were folded cross-wise upon his bandaged chest, but it was not just the Pharaoh's table-top throne that had everyone staring. It was the Pharaoh's face.

It was grey no longer. The skin was powdered a pinkish-white. His eyes were outlined with elegant black lines, along with a becoming shade of blue. Red lipstick adorned his ancient lips and his cheeks were

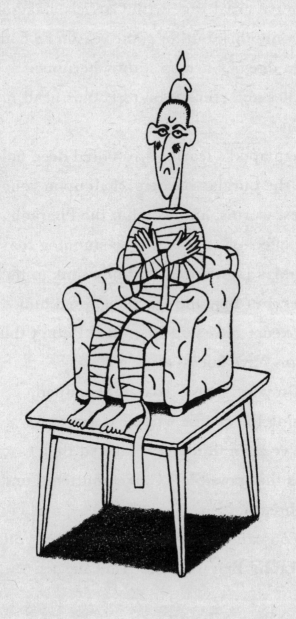

lightly rouged. Sennapod had evidently been having a great time with Carrie's make-up. Not only this, but for some reason he had taken one of Carrie's stubby perfumed candles and stuck it on top of his head, alight.

Sennapod's fearful eyes bored deep holes into the burglar-bashers. 'Fall upon your knees, worms, and worship the Pharaoh!' The effect of all this was so stunning that Mr and Mrs Lightspeed dutifully sank to their knees, but Ben and Carrie ignored him.

'Excuse me,' said Ben. 'But I don't think worms have knees, do they?'

'On your knees!' roared Sennapod, making the candle wobble dangerously.

'I've been thinking –' started Ben.

'Is that possible?' Carrie muttered under her breath.

'You can't really be an Ancient Egyptian Pharaoh,' Ben went on. 'I mean, it's impossible. Nobody can come back from the dead like that. You can't just un-deadify yourself.'

The Lightspeeds paused and looked at Ben, and then at the Pharaoh. 'You've got to admit, he's got a point,' said Mr Lightspeed.

'I have not told you everything,' began Sennapod haughtily. 'I missed a bit out.'

Carrie began to laugh. 'You missed a bit out? I suppose that was the bit where your fairy godmother came along and sprinkled you with stardust . . .'

Sennapod leaped to his feet, or at least he tried to. Since he was already on top of the dining-table, when he jumped up his head hit the ceiling with a skull-cracking thump. The perfumed candle went out at once, but the hot wax was squidged hard against the ceiling and stuck there. Sennapod then sat down so quickly and so hard that one of the table legs broke. The armchair, complete with a very dazed Pharaoh, was suddenly launched forward into thin air. The Lightspeeds threw themselves back against the wall, which was quite difficult for Ben because he still had a guitar on one foot. There they watched helplessly as the big armchair crashed across the room with Sennapod clinging on for dear life. The chair screeched to a halt and Sennapod struggled

to pull himself back into a more regal
position. He pointed a thin, accusing finger
at Carrie.

'Is she always like this?' he exploded. 'She
should be thrown into the cobra-pit!'

'That's what I say,' agreed Ben,
beginning to quite like this crusty old
Pharaoh. Mrs Lightspeed
moved protectively in
front of her daughter.

'Now, you listen here.
You might be a
Pharaoh but I
won't have you
talking to Carrie
like that. What's
more, Ben is right.
People can't un-deadify themselves, or
whatever he said, so kindly explain yourself
– and the candle.'

Then it was Ben's turn again. 'When

Pharaohs were mummified, the priests cut out the lungs, liver, and other stomach bits and put them into, well, sort of jam-jars.'

'There's no need to go into detail,' said Mr Lightspeed, green-faced. 'We haven't had breakfast yet.'

'Well, they did,' Ben went on. 'They had to get the brain out too and that was *really* difficult. They'd get a long piece of wire with a hook on one end and pull your brain out down your nostrils –'

'BEN!'

'All I'm saying *is*: how come Sennapod can wander around if all his insides are missing and he's got no brain?'

This very astute question had all the Lightspeeds looking enquiringly at the Pharaoh. Carrie gingerly felt how large her skull was and then how tiny her small and delicate nostrils were. She winced.

At this point Rustbucket, the Lightspeeds'

ginger cat, trotted into the room. Although the cat had never met Sennapod before, she went directly to him and jumped on to his lap. The Pharaoh smiled as he felt the cat's warm and comforting fur beneath his gnarled fingers. Rustbucket pushed her head under Sennapod's chin, then curled up on his lap and began purring loudly. Somehow the cat's friendliness made Sennapod feel a bit stronger.

'The priests knew I was dying. One of them had invented a new method of mummification that left the body whole. It meant I would be perfect when I reached the Land of the Dead, but the process had to be started before I was actually dead.'

'You were buried alive!' shouted Carrie. 'Yuk! Cree-PEE!'

'I was in a coma. There was only darkness. I had no idea of time. One year, a thousand years – it was all the same. It was

like being asleep – until
the coffin was opened.'

'Who opened it?'
asked Mrs Lightspeed.

Sennapod's face
clouded angrily.

'Miserable maggots
who should be
squeezed slowly
until –'

'Yes, yes,' she quickly interrupted. 'I
suppose it could be true. You certainly look
as if you've been dead for thousands of years
. . . doesn't explain the candle though,' she
added, gazing up at the ceiling once more.

'How come you speak English?' Carrie
suddenly demanded. 'You should be
speaking Ancient Egyptian.'

Sennapod sniffed regally. 'I'm a Pharaoh.
I'm a god. I can do anything I wish.
Anyhow – I've been stuck in an English

museum for seventy years, listening to fools come and go. I've learned a lot.'

Carrie was still not satisfied. 'Well, why have you used up all my make-up and how are you going to get my candle back down and what were you doing up on that table?'

This barrage of questions was too much for Sennapod. He was still immensely tired. His whole body seemed to crumple into the armchair. He fought to keep his eyes on this strange family from another world. 'I don't know. It's all too . . .'

 His head fell to one side and his eyes closed. Rustbucket gave an angry mew and sat up straight and alert,

looking for all the world as if she was guarding the Pharaoh.

'He's dead!' shouted Ben, glaring at his sister. 'You and all your clever-clever questions. I always knew you'd question someone to death one day!'

'That's enough, Ben,' said Mr Lightspeed. 'He's sleeping, that's all. He's still very weak.' He tucked a blanket round the mummy. Sennapod's head jerked several times. His old lips smacked together and gargantuan snores battered the walls. Even the windows rattled.

Mrs Lightspeed beckoned everyone through to the kitchen, where they could at least hear each other. She filled the kettle and began to make a very early breakfast, while Ben tried to explain the business with the candle.

'They used to put perfumed wax on top of their heads,' he said. 'It would melt in the heat and the perfume would dribble down their faces. They thought it made them smell nice.'

'Yuk!' said Carrie.

Mr Lightspeed grinned at them both. 'It's a good idea if you ask me. I bet he'd think it was just as strange to shove deodorant up your armpits! Anyway,' he went on thoughtfully, 'it seems that a four-thousand-year-old Pharaoh with a thing about worms and sticking candles on his head has come to stay with us. What are we going to do now?'

5 The Search Continues

'He can't just have vanished,' said
Grimstone to Professor Jelly in the museum
cafeteria the following morning. They'd had
a miserable night, getting thoroughly
soaked, searching the streets until half past
three before giving up. To make matters
worse, Professor Jelly had got a puncture on
the way home and had only crawled into
bed at four fifteen. At least his headache had
gone.

'Somebody must have seen him, taken
him in maybe, looked after him.' Grimstone
pushed a coin into the coffee machine and
pressed a button. A plastic cup clattered into
place and a thick brown sludge spilled into
it. Grimstone sniffed it in disgust. 'Hot
chocolate,' he scowled. 'I hate the stuff.'

'But you pressed the button for hot

chocolate,' said Jelly. 'I saw you.'

'What do you expect? If I press the black coffee button, which is what I want, do you think I get black coffee? Of course not. This stupid machine gives me tea. If I press the tea button you'd think I'd get coffee, but no, I get tomato soup. I thought if I pressed the chocolate button I certainly wouldn't get chocolate, but I *might* get the black coffee I want.'

Professor Jelly felt his headache about to come back. He couldn't take all this in. '*I* like hot chocolate,' he muttered, taking the cup from Grimstone and sipping it. 'How are we going to find Sennapod?'

'He can't have gone far, and he's going to stick out like a sore thumb in all those bandages. We shall have to hunt him down.'

An idea occurred to Professor Jelly. 'What about that film? Where those men go around looking for ghosts and trapping them in a special box.'

'You mean *Ghostbusters*.'

'Maybe there are people who catch Ancient Egyptians,' suggested the professor. Grimstone considered this.

'It's possible. What do you think they'd be called?'

'Mummybusters? Pharaoh-finders? Look

in *Yellow Pages*.'

Together they skimmed through all the telephone directories they could muster, but it was hopeless. Then they wondered about hiring a private detective, but quickly decided against the idea. They couldn't afford a detective, and supposing they did hire one and the detective found out about the treasure? No, they had to keep this thing to themselves.

Grimstone slapped a fist into the palm of his hand. 'Got it! The police! Why didn't I think of it before? The police are bound to have picked him up. Nobody can wander around the streets at night dressed like Sennapod. The police will have picked him up and put him in an cell overnight for

safe-keeping. Come on!'

Grimstone's tiny moped could hardly cope with two riders at one sitting. Jelly's feet trailed along the road and the speed they made would hardly have done credit to a turbocharged sixteen-valve tortoise. The moped hiccuped past the MISTER FREEZEE van at one end of the street and eventually phutted to a halt outside the police station. They hurried in.

Wattle, the desk sergeant, raised his

eyebrows questioningly. 'Yes, gentlemen?'

'We're looking for a Pharaoh,' said Grimstone, getting straight to the point. 'Might have come in last night. Have you got one?'

'Pharaoh?' replied Sergeant Wattle, scanning the list of pick-ups brought in during the night. 'Can't say there's a Mr Pharaoh here. Got a Miss Fairseat – she was picked up last night, and there's a drunken fairy from some fancy-dress party. What does he look like? Any distinctive features?'

'He's covered in bandages from head to toe.'

'Oh? Been in an accident, has he?'

'Not exactly. Look, have you got him or not?' demanded Grimstone impatiently. Sergeant Wattle shook his head.

'Sorry, gentlemen. By the way, if that's your moped outside, you do realize that one of you hasn't got a crash-helmet? It's against the law to ride a mo-*ped*, motor-*cycle* or any two-wheeled motor-*vehicle* without a crash-helmet.'

Grimstone turned to Jelly and shrugged. 'Sorry, Jelly, looks like you'll have to walk.' Grimstone pulled on his helmet and rode away, leaving the professor gazing after him. Professor Jelly sighed and began to trudge back down the long street. This was absolutely typical. Why did everything awkward have to happen to him? Why couldn't he have a decent break for a change?

Professor Jelly glanced at the picture of ice-lollies on the side of the MISTER FREEZEE van as he passed, and his steps faltered. Why not? He fished some coins from his pocket and went to the counter. 'I'll have a triple cone – chocolate, pistachio and strawberry – with three flaky-bars, please.'

'You look like you need it,' said Tony Lightspeed, squeezing a big dollop of strawberry ice-cream into a cone. 'Having a bad day?'

The professor nodded. 'And it's only just started,' he grumbled. 'My friend's just gone off on his moped and left me to walk. It's miles to where I'm going.'

'Must be one of those days,' said Mr Lightspeed sympathetically. 'I've been having trouble myself. You can't imagine what I've got waiting for me when I get home.'

Professor Jelly licked his ice-cream and shook his head.

'An Ancient Egyptian Pharaoh,' announced Mr Lightspeed. 'Now, look! You've dropped your ice-cream on your foot!'

But Professor Jelly didn't care about his ice-cream. He gripped the counter with his pudgy hands. 'Tell me more about this Pharaoh,' he suggested slyly . . .

6 Where's the Asses' Milk?

While Sennapod dozed, with Rustbucket still on guard, Mrs Lightspeed worked away at her old, white dressing-gown. She had been altering it all morning, making the bottom longer and letting the sleeves down. It was almost ready.

Ben and Carrie had been busy too. They had found a picture in one of Ben's books of a Pharaoh, sitting on his throne. 'He's wearing make-up,' sniffed Carrie. 'So that's why Sennapod borrowed all my stuff.'

'I don't understand it,' said Ben. 'How come the Pharaohs could look so good, but

when you put it on –'

'Ben!' warned their mother, and he hurriedly studied the picture once more. On his head the Pharaoh wore a tall double crown, with the head of the cobra-goddess, to show that he ruled over both Upper and Lower Egypt. On his chin was the ceremonial false beard, always worn by the Pharaohs.

Carrie and Ben set about copying them. The beard was easily made from a toilet-roll tube and some thin elastic, but the crown was far more complicated. Carrie bent some card round to make the main shape. Ben added a kitchen-roll tube – leaving a pile of floppy kitchen towel all over the floor – and topped it with a tennis-ball. Then he lifted the crown from the table and put it on.

'What does it look like?' he asked.

Carrie studied it from several angles. 'I think it looks like some wonky cardboard with a tube up the middle and a tennis-ball on top.'

Mrs Lightspeed glanced up from her sewing. 'It will be fine when you've painted it.'

'The cobra-goddess is missing,' Carrie pointed out. Ben rushed upstairs to his room and came dashing back, waving a big rubber snake. He grabbed the scissors, snipped off the snake's head, plastered one end with glue and slapped it on the front of the crown. Carrie eyed it with distaste.

'I loathe snakes,' she muttered.

'How do you manage to look in the mirror so much, then?' Ben asked, pushing the cobra-head back into place as it slid down the crown for the third time.

'Let me do it, Ben. You're hopeless.' Carrie used the stapler to punch a few staples through the rubber. 'There. All it takes is a bit of intelligence.'

'Don't you two ever stop arguing?' sighed Mrs Lightspeed. 'Look, I've finished the royal robe. What do you think?' She studied the children's faces. 'I know it's not perfect, but it's better than nothing. It will look better when it's on. Let's see if Sennapod's awake yet.'

The Pharaoh stirred in the armchair. He snorted several times, wiggled his nose and slowly opened his eyes. He was certainly surprised by what he saw. Carrie was holding out the crown rather awkwardly. Ben had the beard, quickly coloured with

felt-tips, and Mrs Lightspeed stood there
holding out the royal dressing-robe, smiling
sheepishly.

Sennapod straightened his aged back and
took the crown from Carrie with both hands.
He lifted it slowly to his head. It fitted
rather well. 'We've still got to paint it the
right colours,' Carrie pointed out. For a
moment the Pharaoh's black eyes lost their
stony glint.

'Thank you,' he said loftily. 'Maybe you are not worms after all. Perhaps you are only small animals of some kind, mice perhaps, or small rats.'

'You are most kind, Your Majesty,' smiled Mrs Lightspeed, giving a little curtsy. 'Now, I think it's time you had a bath. Then you can try on your robe.' She spoke so briskly that Sennapod listened in astonished silence. 'Come on, this way.' Mrs Lightspeed pulled the Pharaoh from the armchair and pushed him up the stairs in front of her, with Rustbucket trotting at his heels – the two now seemed to be inseparable.

Mrs Lightspeed showed Sennapod the little bathroom, gave him a clean towel, put in the plug, turned on the tap and then pulled the door shut. She had taken barely five steps when the door was whisked open and Sennapod put his scowling head round

the door-frame. He fixed Mrs Lightspeed
with a very imperious eye.

'Where are you going?' he demanded.
'You must come and bath me, and Carrie
too.'

'I *beg* your pardon!' cried Mrs Lightspeed,

shocked from head to toe. 'We shall do no such thing. How dare you!'

Sennapod stepped out into the hallway and glowered back at her. 'How dare *you* speak to the Pharaoh like that! I command that you both be my handmaidens. I am always bathed in asses' milk by my handmaidens.'

Mrs Lightspeed took a deep breath and pushed Sennapod back into the bathroom. 'That was long, long ago. You're a big boy now. You will have to bath yourself. Now, get those stinky bandages off and get on with it.'

She hurried from the bathroom, pulled the door shut and almost ran downstairs. With a sigh of relief, she collapsed into an armchair. Having a Pharaoh in the house was hard work.

All at once a loud cry came from upstairs. 'Where's the asses' milk?' demanded

Sennapod from the top of the stairs. Mrs Lightspeed groaned and looked across at her children, busily painting the Pharaoh's crown.

'Ben, go and chuck a tub of yoghurt into his bath will you, there's a dear.'

7 Sennapod the Champ

Sennapod looked much better after a long bath, although when he slapped some yoghurt under each arm, it did feel a bit odd. After pulling on Mrs Lightspeed's altered dressing-gown, he searched through his ancient bandages. Shortly he found a flattened piece of parchment. He looked at it intently before glancing around the room. He crossed to the big mirror and carefully pushed the ancient treasure map out of sight behind it. Then he noticed his reflection.

At 4,600 years old, he was in good shape. He tried on the ceremonial toilet-tube beard, but he had never come across elastic before. The beard was accidentally catapulted across the room. It scored a direct hit on a small flowerpot, sending it crashing into the

toilet bowl, where it floated about rather prettily.

At his second attempt, the beard knocked the bubble-mix jar into the bath. The third time, it bounced off the ceiling and rocketed down into the frothy bubbles that were already rising over the sides of the tub.

Sennapod swished his hand around,

searching for the lost beard and creating
even bigger bubbles. Eventually, he fished
out a very soggy piece of card with a dollop
of yoghurt on one end. He held it to his chin,
but it didn't look right at all. Never mind,
he'd order the slaves downstairs to make
him another.

Sennapod shouted from behind the closed
door. 'Make way for Sennapod, He Whose
Name Shall Rumble et cetera, the Pharaoh
desires to leave his bath.' He stopped and

waited. Was *nobody* going to open the door for his royal personage? Where were those slaves? He tried again. 'Make way for Sennapod, Lord of Serpents, Master of Hippos, Osiris on . . .'

The door was thrown open by Carrie and her mother. 'Do you have to stand up here shouting?' demanded Carrie. 'And why are you talking to the door?'

'I was waiting for a worm to open it,' said Sennapod pompously.

'Oh, we've gone back to being worms, have we? We're not your slaves, you know.'

'But you *are*,' insisted Sennapod. 'You must be my slaves.'

'Oh yes? Why?' Carrie folded her arms defiantly. Sennapod's reply was very simple.

'Because I am the Pharaoh and *all* people are my slaves.' This shut Carrie up long enough for Mrs Lightspeed to admire her dressing-gown.

'You do look nice, Senny. Those sleeves are just the right length – but what about that lovely beard?' The Pharaoh held out a handful of mushy card. 'Never mind, Ben can soon make a new one.' Her face took on a bewildered squint as she watched a tidal wave of bubbles creep up behind Sennapod. 'Oh dear, I think you may have used a bit too much bubble-mix. Carrie, take Senny downstairs . . .'

'Do NOT call me Senny!' hissed the Pharaoh.

'Don't call us worms, then,' Mrs Lightspeed suggested, trying to load handfuls of bubbles back into the bath.

At the top of the stairs, Sennapod paused and listened. Weird bleeping and blooping noises came from Ben's bedroom. The Pharaoh went across and poked his ancient head round the door. In an instant he was transfixed by a scene of such utter wonder, he almost fainted with pleasure.

Ben's eyes were glued to his TV screen, where strange little creatures were whizzing around: running, leaping, fighting – all to the accompaniment of magical sounds. Ben's fingers flicked across his control pad. Suddenly a mournful drone came from the TV and Ben sighed. 'Rats! I've died!'

Sennapod stepped into the room and spoke in an awed whisper. 'What is this wonderful machine?'

'This? It's my Mega-CD. I'm playing a game called Magnificent Marvin.' Ben held up the control pad. 'Want a go?' Sennapod sat down quickly and grabbed the pad. Ben hastily explained all the different buttons, but the Pharaoh just wanted to get going. Ben started the program. Within thirty seconds Sennapod had died three times. He started again, reached Level One, then Level Two. Ben couldn't believe how

quickly he'd picked it up. Within ten
minutes Sennapod was on Level Seven and
Ben was hopping up and down.

'It's not fair – I've only ever got to Level
Five.' All the same, he was fascinated by the
skill and ease with which this Ancient
Egyptian was racing through the game.

Soon the TV gave a whoop of triumph and a message flashed on-screen: WELL DONE, SENNAPOD! YOU ARE THE CHAMPION! CONGRATULATIONS FROM MAGNIFICENT MARVIN.

The Pharaoh sighed with pleasure and handed the control pad back to Ben, who was quite speechless. 'Thank you, that was good.' Sennapod got as far as the door, then stopped. A small frown added even more wrinkles to his brow. He turned back to Ben. 'This Magnificent Marvin,' he asked. 'Was he a Pharaoh who came after me?'

8 The Hunters Close In

'I feel stupid,' said Professor Jelly, trying to yank the tweed skirt over his knobbly knees. 'This is really itchy. I don't see why I had to dress up as a woman.'

'I told you,' grunted Grimstone. 'We don't want MISTER FREEZEE to recognize you. Remember that he's seen you once already. *Please* try and keep still, Jelly! How do you expect me to keep an eye on the van with you joggling about?'

The two men were sitting on Grimstone's moped, some way up the road from the ice-cream van. When Professor Jelly had told Grimstone of his good luck in finding Sennapod, they had put a rapid plan into action. For the last three hours they had sat there watching MISTER FREEZEE. Grimstone was holding up a newspaper.

There was a carefully torn hole in the centre through which he was trying to watch the van.

Professor Jelly went on fidgeting nervously. He'd left his sweets in his own clothes and he really missed them. He felt very self-conscious wearing a lady's tweed suit, a long blonde wig and a little hat with a feather perched on top. 'You might have let me have a beard and moustache,' he complained.

'There weren't any left in the Disguise Shop, and stop wriggling. I think he's packing up.' Grimstone pressed the starter on the moped and prepared to follow the van. Sure enough, MISTER FREEZEE began to move up the street, and Grimstone followed at a discreet distance. Within seconds there was a startled shriek in his left ear and he almost swerved on to the pavement.

'My hat's blown off!' squeaked Professor Jelly. 'Don't go so fast. It will be the wig next – it's twisting round. I can't see a thing. Stop!'

'I can't stop, you fool. We'll lose the van. Just hold on to your wig, will you?'

Grimstone tried to shut his ears to the non-stop moans, groans, squeaks and squawks that continued to come from the professor as he fought with his wig, his skirt, his shoes and his balance.

Finally, the van stopped outside the Lightspeeds' house. The moped screeched to a halt at a safe distance. Professor Jelly wrestled angrily with Grimstone's back and the moped before he managed to disentangle himself from the seat. He went stomping off down the road to find his hat. By the time he got back, Grimstone was once more stuck behind his newspaper. 'He's just gone into Number 27,' he hissed.

Professor Jelly plonked himself back on the moped and sulkily asked if Grimstone had seen Sennapod yet. Grimstone eyed his partner. 'No, but you've smudged your lipstick. It looks as if someone has whacked you in the mouth.'

'I hate this game!' Professor Jelly stamped one shoe angrily and the heel slid between the slats of a drain cover. It stuck fast. He tugged on his leg, but it was well and truly jammed, so he gave an almighty heave. The heel broke off, sending him toppling backwards off the moped. Professor Jelly fell in the road and his blonde wig fell in the gutter. He grabbed it quickly and pulled it back on to his head, only to discover that he now had half a mouldy banana skin squashed between the wig and his bald skull. He was about to scream with one

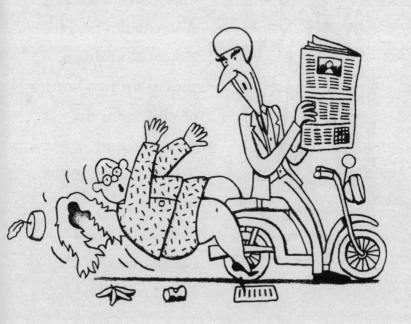

hundred per cent frustration, when Grimstone stiffened and pointed a finger through the hole in the paper. 'Look, look!'

The door of Number 27 had opened, and there was the Pharaoh himself. Sennapod

stood in his robe and crown and beard, gazing majestically up and down Templeton Terrace. He looked every inch a king of Ancient Egypt. He slowly bent down, picked up two bottles of milk from the doorstep and disappeared back indoors.

'Bingo!' cried Grimstone. 'We've found him. The

treasure is as good as ours now!'

'Does that mean we can go home?' asked Professor Jelly, and in answer to this Grimstone started up the moped and they set off once more.

'What do we do next?' shouted the professor, clinging to his hat and wig. 'We can't just go in there and kidnap him.'

Grimstone chuckled quietly. 'Of course we can't. I have a much better plan. We are going to get Sennapod to come right back to the museum itself, when nobody else is around. And once he's there, he'll be ours and we can do what we like with him. We shall not only get the treasure map, we'll have a real Pharaoh. Imagine the money we can make, showing him to the public!'

'But how on earth will you get him to come back?' demanded the professor.

'Easy as pie. This is what we'll do . . .'

9 All About Tiddles

The last person to expect a postcard the following morning was Sennapod. After all, he had died over four thousand years earlier and had never left a forwarding address. He was very pleased to get a postcard, because it took everyone's attention away from the toaster in the kitchen.

Sennapod was very impressed with the toaster. You put in cold bread and it popped

up a little later, all hot and toasty.
Sennapod's early morning cup of tea had
gone cold, so he thought he'd warm that up
and he poured it into the toaster. There was
an almighty BANG! a cloud of acrid smoke
and all the lights went out.

'Well done,' said Carrie icily.

For the first time, even the Pharaoh
seemed a bit embarrassed. He frowned
angrily at the toaster and pointed an
accusing finger. 'Worm!'

Ben groaned. 'You can't call a toaster a
worm,' he said, and it was at this
point that the post arrived.
Everyone admired the picture,
which showed the Great Pyramid
of Cheops, although Sennapod
complained that it looked
very tatty now.

'What does the card say?'
asked Carrie nosily, and

the Pharaoh turned it over. On the back, to their astonishment, was a message scrawled in hieroglyphs. Sennapod scowled as he read.

'What is it?' asked Mr Lightspeed. 'It's not about double glazing, is it?'

'Spelling mistakes,' growled the Pharaoh, but then he gave a strangled cry. 'They've got my cat!' The Lightspeeds looked at each other. Sennapod was certainly full of surprises.

'I didn't know you had a cat,' said Ben.

'His name is Crusher of Worms.'

'Crusher of Worms!' Carrie was disgusted. 'You can't call a cat Crusher of Worms!'

Sennapod turned on her. 'Do you argue with everyone? Crusher of Worms is his royal name. I usually call him Tiddles.'

Mr Lightspeed turned the card over in his hands. 'But who's got your cat, and why is it so important? Is there something you haven't told us?'

Sennapod looked at each Lightspeed in turn, thinking hard. They were the only people he knew in this strange world, the only people he felt he might be able to trust.

'The Pharaoh is always buried with great treasure. Mine was hidden near by . . .'

'Wow – like Tutankhamun!' said Ben.

'Do not interrupt when the Pharaoh is speaking! The royal graves have always been plundered by grave-robbers. It was decided to hide my treasure horde and leave a secret map with my body, so that the gods would know where to look.'

'Wow – a treasure map!' cried Ben, making Carrie wince.

'Do you think you could stop shouting "wow"? You're beginning to sound like a fire engine on red alert.'

Mrs Lightspeed sat Sennapod down. He'd had quite a shock, though whether it was the postcard or the toaster was difficult to tell. 'So the men who sent this card want to exchange Tiddles for the map?' Sennapod nodded. Mrs Lightspeed shrugged. 'I don't see what all the fuss is about. You keep the map and let them keep the cat. After all, it is only a cat.'

Sennapod erupted from his chair. '*Only* a cat!' he roared. 'The *royal* cat! *My* cat! A god – like me! Tiddles is sacred. Do you know what happens to those who dare harm a cat?' The Lightspeeds huddled together, staring at the furious Pharaoh.

'Death!' spat Sennapod.

A ghastly silence fell upon the room.

Ben cleared his throat. 'You'd like Tiddles back, then?'

'It must be done,' growled the Pharaoh. 'My cat is sacred to me, to the gods and the people of Egypt.' He sat down heavily and held his head in his hands. Rustbucket prowled the room, as if she expected to find tomb-robbers behind every armchair. Mr Lightspeed gently patted the Pharaoh's shoulder.

'Don't worry. We'll get Tiddles back. Now, where is he?'

'At the museum,' said Sennapod, glancing at the card.

Suddenly, it all began to fall into place. 'The museum,' said Mr Lightspeed. 'Is that where you came from? I was near there when I found you. Of course! They've got a big Ancient Egyptian collection. Something odd is going on.' The family crowded round the table, encouraging Sennapod.

'I must go to the museum,' he insisted.

'We'll come with you,' said Mrs Lightspeed.

'Great!' Ben dashed off to get his jacket.

'Not you two,' said his mother. 'You stay here, just in case. And it's no good arguing, so don't start. Dad and I will go with Sennapod and get Tiddles back.'

The three adults went to the door. Mr and Mrs Lightspeed put on their coats and Sennapod put on his crown. 'You are kind to help me,' he said. 'Maybe, maybe . . .'

'Yes?' prompted Mrs Lightspeed with a tiny smile.

'Maybe you are . . . baboons,' he offered.

'Baboons?' chorused Mr and Mrs Lightspeed.

'It's better than worms or mice,' Sennapod quickly pointed out, as they hurried up the road towards the museum.

Rustbucket followed, close on Sennapod's heels, and as they marched up the road they were joined by more and more cats, padding silently, unobserved by Mr and Mrs Lightspeed.

Ben and Carrie stood by the front door. 'Will they be OK?' Carrie asked. Ben pulled on his jacket.

'There's only one way to find out,' he said. 'We'll follow them without them ever knowing. Come on!'

10 Trapped!

'There are three of them!'
panicked Professor Jelly,
peering out through the
museum windows. 'And
they've got an army of
cats with them!'

'Cats?' snarled
Grimstone. 'What use are
they? I don't care if
they've brought their
guinea-pigs and goldfish with them. We're
going to get that treasure, Jelly! Sennapod's
the one we want. I shall have to get rid of
Mr and Mrs Freezee.'

Grimstone's eyes raced around the
deserted room until his wicked gaze fell
upon the display of old-fashioned weapons.
Taking pride of place was a massive

blunderbuss, whose long barrel opened out
like the mouth of a great trombone.
Grimstone seized the antiquated weapon
and the little pouch of gunpowder beside it.
He looked for ammunition, but couldn't find
anything suitable. Never mind, those stupid
Lightspeeds would never know the gun
wasn't loaded!

'We've got to fix those other two,' shouted Grimstone. 'I have a nice little surprise planned for them. Tell Sennapod I'll be waiting in the store-room.' Grimstone vanished with the blunderbuss.

As Sennapod and the Lightspeeds came through the revolving doors, Professor Jelly stepped out of the shadows to welcome his victims. He tried to force a cheery smile, even though his insides had tied themselves into tiny, nervous knots. 'Well, well, we meet again!' he simpered.

'You!' cried Mr Lightspeed, recognizing Jelly at once.

'Yes – me!' Jelly squeaked, as if even he was surprised to find himself in such a

situation. He was about to say more, but was cut short by Sennapod.

'Where is Crusher of Worms, you piece of maggot-flesh? Give him to me at once!'

'Oh, you are in a hurry,' teased the professor. 'I don't know why – you seem to have plenty of cats of your own.'

Sennapod and his two bodyguards looked behind for the first time. 'Great heavens!' cried Mr Lightspeed. 'Where did they come from? There must be dozens of them.'

The Pharaoh smiled grimly. 'I am their true master. They follow me. They are my slaves, like both of you.' Rustbucket pushed her head against his leg as he spoke. He turned back to Jelly. 'Where is Crusher of Worms?' he repeated.

'Where is the map?' giggled Jelly, trying to sound ruthless, but behaving more like a piece of damp cotton wool. Sennapod pulled a parchment from inside his robe and held it up. 'I must have my cat first, and may the treasure bring you nothing but unhappiness and disaster, you son of a scorpion; grandson of a three-legged camel; father of a million house-flies; daughter of a centipede, mother of a six-humped . . .'

'I think you're getting a bit muddled,' whispered Mr Lightspeed, and they followed Professor Jelly down to the store-room.

A musty smell filled the grey air. It was a big room, piled high with empty mummy-cases, old statues, paintings, pottery, masks and costumes and all-sorts. As soon as they entered the room, Grimstone leaped out behind them, waving the blunderbuss dangerously and slamming the door shut. Rustbucket and her army of cats were left scratching helplessly on the far side of the door.

'Lady and gentlemen!' cried Grimstone with a crazy leer. 'We really did not expect

three of you. How unfair! And all those cats!
But never mind, I do believe we can sort
things out.' He waved the gun at the
Lightspeeds. 'Jelly, we shall have to get
these two out of the way. You fetch those old
bandages and wrap up Mr Freezee, nice and
tight. Sennapod here can wrap his missus.'
Grimstone pointed at a big pile of bandages
left over from earlier mummy-investigations.

Sennapod stiffened. 'I shall not do it,' he said snootily.

'Oh yes you will. If you don't, I'll shoot them both,' said Grimstone simply. Mrs Lightspeed went very pale.

'You'd better do it,' she said quietly to the Pharaoh.

'What a sensible woman!' laughed Grimstone. 'I have never met such a sensible woman!'

'That's probably because no sensible woman would ever go near you,' Mrs Lightspeed managed to say before she disappeared beneath a swathe of ancient bandages. Their mouths were covered so they couldn't shout for help. Their arms were pinioned against their bodies. Only their eyes peeped out helplessly.

Grimstone found it all hilarious. 'I'm so clever, Jelly! And I've just had a wonderful thought. I know exactly where to keep these

two mummies safe and sound. Open the
coffins!' The old mummy-cases were thrown
open and Mr and Mrs Lightspeed bundled
inside. The lids were slammed shut.

'There!' cried Grimstone, turning to the
Pharaoh and levelling the old blunderbuss at
his ancient heart. 'Now, let's have that
treasure map.'

11 Ye Gods!

Grimstone and Jelly were so busy playing about with mummy-cases and bandages that they didn't notice the store-room door quietly inch open. Ben and Carrie peeped round the edge, with Rustbucket pushing her small head between them. The two children crawled silently into the room and hid behind a pile of packing-cases. One by one, the cats followed and spread themselves around.

Ben's heart was thundering away like a talking-drum, beating out an urgent message. He could almost hear it saying 'Help! What are we going to do? Help! What are we going to do?' over and over again. Carrie must have heard it too.

'What are we going to do?' she echoed. 'He's got a gun!'

'Tell me about it!' hissed Ben. 'We can't just sit here and do nothing.' He glanced at the packing-cases. Some were lying on their sides. They were stuffed with paper and straw, and inside were several masks of the Ancient Egyptian Gods.

Ben grinned and quietly pulled out a very impressive head of Sebek, the crocodile-god. He passed it to Carrie and she put it on.

'Big improvement!' he muttered. 'It suits you.' Next he pulled out the falcon-headed god, Horus. 'This will do me nicely,' he whispered and promptly crawled off to the far end of the store-room. His heart was pounding even harder and all it seemed to shout now was 'Help! Help! Help! Help!' Ben struggled to overcome his fear. This was their only chance. He cleared his throat and stood up.

'I am the God Horus!' cried Ben, feeling his knees trembling. 'Throw down your weapon. It is useless to resist!'

'Horus!' Sennapod was overjoyed. 'You have come to my aid!'

Grimstone and Jelly stared stupefied at the god. 'What is it?' asked Jelly hoarsely.

'Don't panic,' warned Grimstone, his eyes flitting back to the parchment in Sennapod's wrinkled hand. 'Give me the map!' he commanded, but a cry from behind made them whirl round.

'I am Sebek, the crocodile-god!' yelled Carrie, hoping she sounded as fierce as she looked. 'Release your prisoners or I will chew you up and spit out your bones like – um – grape pips.' She grinned to herself. She liked that bit about the grape pips.

Professor Jelly went to pieces. 'The gods are attacking us!' he screamed. 'It's The Curse of Anubis! We should never have opened the coffin!' Grimstone grabbed Jelly's arm.

'Get a grip on yourself, you fool. Find me some ammunition for this gun, quick!' He poured gunpowder down the huge barrel, while Jelly frantically searched for something suitable, but all he could find in his pockets were handfuls of chocolates. He threw them down the barrel.

'Stand back!' yelled Grimstone, wildly aiming the gun at Sebek. There was an enormous bang, smoke puffed grandly from the blunderbuss and the crocodile hastily ducked as a swarm of gaily wrapped

chocolates buzzed angrily overhead.

'Yee-hah!' cried Grimstone, rapidly
reloading. 'Death to the gods!' He spun
round like a gunslinger, grinning madly.
'Eat chocolates, sucker!' he bellowed and
fired at Horus. Thirty-eight chocolates
peppered the wall behind Ben's head. The
soft-centred ones made a very satisfying
SPLAT noise, and stuck there.

For a short while, it seemed that Grimstone was back in charge, but he had forgotten about Sennapod, Rustbucket and the forty cats. The Pharaoh threw open the mummy-cases and by the time Grimstone and Jelly saw what he was up to, it was too late.

Out of the coffins stepped Mr and Mrs Lightspeed, half bandaged but able to stagger about. They came stumbling towards the two would-be robbers. From either end of the store-room came Sebek and Horus. Sennapod was rather startled to see that Horus was a lot shorter than he expected and was wearing Ben's jeans and trainers. From all sides, cats stuck out their angry heads, fur on end, tails flicking and tiny teeth glinting.

'Run for it!' yelled Grimstone, throwing his gun to the ground. The two men made for the door, hotly pursued by one Ancient

Egyptian Pharaoh, two not-so-ancient
Egyptian gods, two mummies (or one
mummy and one daddy), and forty-one cats.

The thieves didn't get far. Rustbucket
quickly put herself in their path and they

both tripped and fell in a sprawling, whining heap. Sennapod, who had armed himself with the blunderbuss, strode over and glared down at them. He was quickly joined by all the Lightspeeds, and they spoke as one.

'Worms!' they chorused.

Carrie and Ben threw off their masks and gave a whoop of triumph. They pulled the bandages from their parents, and there were hugs all round. In the middle of this, the forty cats moved silently to the sides of the room, forming a sort of guard of honour. Rustbucket trotted up between them, tail in the air, leading the most beautiful cat the Lightspeeds had ever set eyes on. His coat

was a deep blue-black and he wore a gold
ear-ring in one ear. His face was slender,
elegant and aristocratic. He regarded
everything and everyone with two imperious
green eyes.

'Tiddles!' cried a rapturous Pharaoh, and
the four-thousand-year-old moggy leaped
into his master's arms. A monstrous purr

filled the room. When, at length, the Lightspeeds were able to tear their eyes away from Crusher of Worms, they noticed that all the other cats had quietly disappeared – all except Rustbucket.

'I sent them home,' explained the Pharaoh. 'Their job was done, and now ours is too.'

That was not strictly correct. Mr Lightspeed had to call the police and it took a while to explain the whole story. Sergeant Wattle was not at all sure he believed Sennapod was a Pharaoh, especially when he realized that his crown was made from kitchen roll and a tennis-ball. However, he was polite and kept his doubts to himself. Grimstone and Jelly were carted off to the police station.

That evening, the Lightspeeds had a celebration. Mrs Lightspeed couldn't get hold of any roast hippo, so they made do

with sausages. They retold their adventures
endlessly until Mr Lightspeed finally
mentioned the treasure. 'I hope you have the
map safe and sound,' he said to Sennapod.

The Pharaoh pulled the parchment from
his robe and his old face creased with a large
smile. 'You may see for yourself,' he said.

122

Mr Lightspeed carefully opened it up. It didn't look like a map at all. There were just a few hieroglyphs squiggled on it.

'This is the map?' he asked.

'No, of course not. It's the bill for all the bandages I was wrapped in. It must have got caught in them when I was being mummified.'

'Then where's the real map?' cried Ben.

Sennapod smiled at them all. It was obvious he wasn't going to say. Instead, he raised his glass of wine. 'A toast to my loyal friends!' he beamed.

'Friends?' repeated Carrie in surprise. 'Does that mean we're humans at last?'

The Pharaoh frowned slightly. 'Almost,' he admitted. He pushed back his chair and rose to his feet. 'Now, I have something very important to do.' Sennapod swept from the room and went upstairs. A few moments later, the Lightspeeds heard a familiar bleeping and blooping coming from Ben's room, quickly followed by a cry of despair.

'Argh! I hate Magnificent Marvin! I've been zapped by the evil Mega-monster!'

Want to keep laughing?
Enjoy even more hysterically funny adventures

14½ Things You Didn't Know About

Jeremy Strong

★ ★

1. He loves eating liquorice.

2. He used to like diving. He once dived from the high board and his trunks came off!

3. He used to play electric violin in a rock band called **THE INEDIBLE CHEESE SANDWICH.**

4. He got a 100-metre swimming certificate when he couldn't even swim.

5. When he was five, he sat on a heater and burnt his bottom.

6. Jeremy used to look after a dog that kept eating his underpants. (No – **NOT** while he was wearing them!)

7. When he was five, he left a basin tap running with the plug in and flooded the bathroom.

8. He can make his ears waggle.

9. He has visited over a thousand schools.

10. He once scored minus ten in an exam! That's ten less than nothing!

11. His hair has gone grey, but his mind hasn't.

12. He'd like to have a pet tiger.

13. He'd like to learn the piano.

14. He has dreadful handwriting.

And a half . . . His favourite hobby is sleeping. He's very good at it.

Ask Jeremy

Of all the books you have written, which one is your favourite?

I loved writing both **KRAZY KOW SAVES THE WORLD – WELL, ALMOST** and **STUFF**, my first book for teenagers. Both these made me laugh out loud while I was writing and I was pleased with the overall result in each case. I also love writing the stories about Nicholas and his daft family – **MY DAD**, **MY MUM**, **MY BROTHER** and so on.

If you couldn't be a writer what would you be?

Well, I'd be pretty fed up for a start, because writing was the one thing I knew I wanted to do from the age of nine onward. But if I DID have to do something else, I would love to be either an accomplished pianist or an artist of some sort. Music and art have played a big part in my whole life and I would love to be involved in them in some way.

What's the best thing about writing stories?

Oh dear – so many things to say here! Getting paid for making things up is pretty high on the list! It's also something you do on your own, inside your own head – nobody can interfere with that. The only boss you have is yourself. And you are creating something that nobody else has made before you. I also love making my readers laugh and want to read more and more.

Did you ever have a nightmare teacher?
(And who was your best ever?)

My nightmare at primary school was Mrs Chappell, long since dead. I knew her secret – she was not actually human. She was a Tyrannosaurus rex in disguise. She taught me for two years when I was in Y5 and Y6, and we didn't like each other at all. My best ever was when I was in Y3 and Y4. Her name was Miss Cox, and she was the one who first encouraged me to write stories. She was brilliant. Sadly, she is long dead too.

When you were a kid you used to play kiss-chase. Did you always do the chasing or did anyone ever chase you?!

I usually did the chasing, but when I got chased, I didn't bother to run very fast! Maybe I shouldn't admit to that! We didn't play kiss-chase at school – it was usually played during holidays. If we had tried playing it at school we would have been in serious trouble. Mind you, I seemed to spend most of my time in trouble of one sort or another, so maybe it wouldn't have mattered that much.